MW00907315

The Sisters from the Stars

witten and illustrated by

Amy Eleanor Heart

Heartspark Press

Olympia, Washington

Published by
Heartspark Press
Olympia, Washington.

ISBN (Hardback) : 978-0-9996730-4-1
ISBN (Paperback): 978-0-9996730-3-4
Library of Congress Control Number: 2018900837

This is a work of fiction. Names, characters, events, and incidents are either the products of the author's imagination or used in a fictitious manner. Any resemblance to actual persons, living or dead, or actual events is purely coincidental. We pinky swear.

For media inquiries, email us at kidlit@heartsparkpress.com.

All snail mail written correspondence should be sent to:

Heartspark Press
PO Box 2659
Olympia, WA 98507

This book is dedicated to my father.

Without his endless love and support,
none of this work would even exist.

I love you, Dad.

See you on the other side of the galaxy.

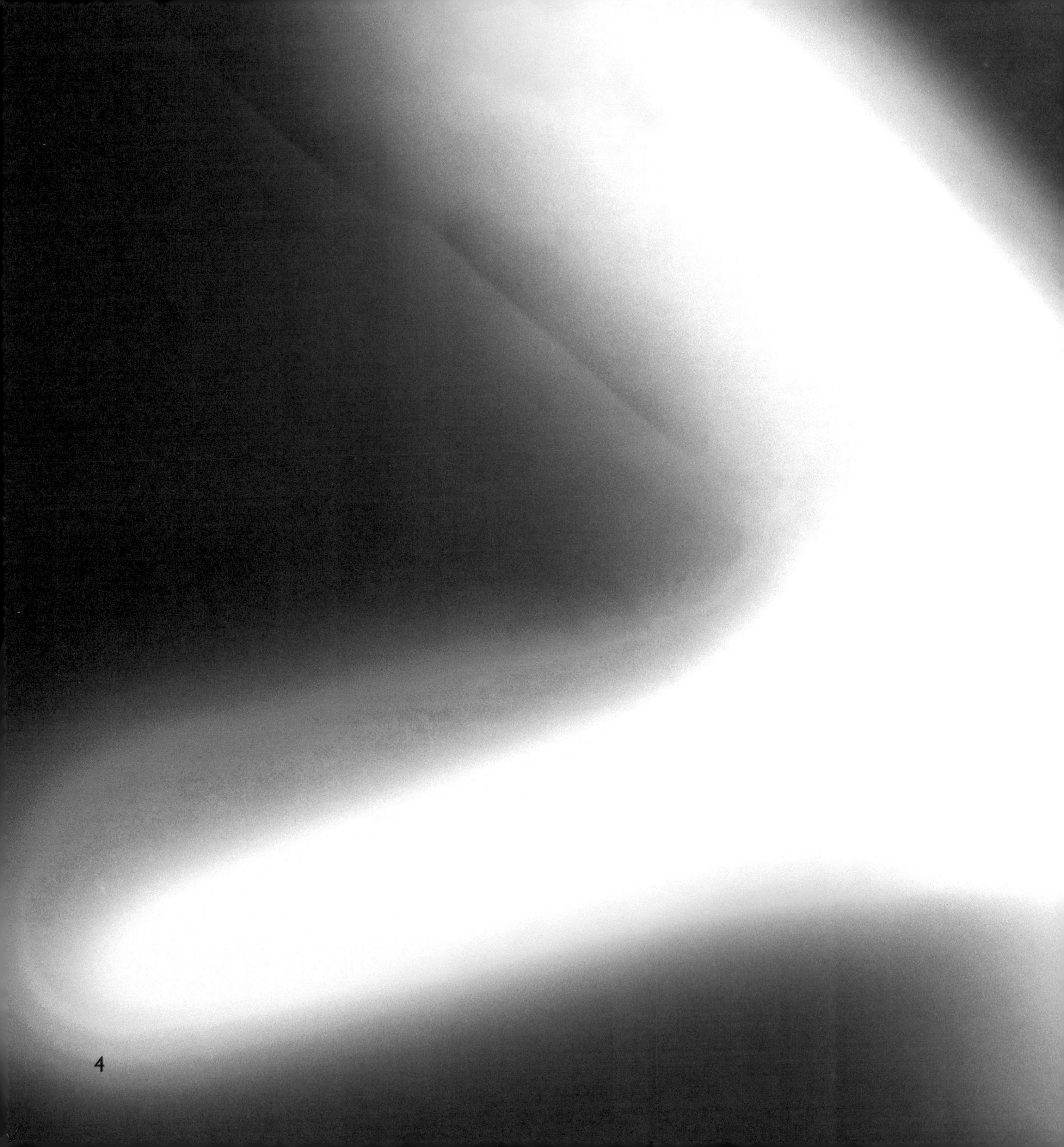

For my Papa
and our Pearl

Once upon a time,
in a star system
sixty-five trillion miles away,
there shined a bright and
beautiful princess
named Hailey.

But Hailey wasn't any ordinary princess. She was a starheart, to be precise. And starhearts looked a lot like human beings—that is to say, if human beings had pink butterfly wings and bold magic wands.

This made Hailey different than anyone she knew, but that didn't matter to her. Hailey loved who she was and everything that she was becoming. But being so different, so unique, came with a cost. She was always lonely —a great loneliness that never seemed to go away.

You see, while Hailey believed everybody she met was beautiful and unique in their own right, she knew deep down the ones she wanted to be with the most—her tribe—were those also struggling to find a place called home. *Girls like her*, she would often tell herself. ***Girls like us.***

There was one particular human that Hailey always wanted to talk with at school. She wasn't entirely sure what their name or pronouns were, but there was something distinctly familiar about them.

Perhaps it was the way this human walked. There was always a gentle kindness with every step they took, despite the overwhelming sadness in their eyes. Maybe it was their light green hair that reminded Hailey of her favorite milkshake: super-sprinty, minty-chippy, chocolate chip swirl. It could have also been the daily doodles on their arms that were filled with dragons, swords, and complex magical incantations.

Either way, Hailey was mesmerized. Amazed? Perplexed, even. If she could only find the courage to talk to this human, who knows what would happen?

MILK

So Hailey tried. Day after day, she tried to muster up her nerve and finally speak. *This will be it! This will be the day!* she whispered to herself while approaching The Milkshake Human. *I'm going to do it. I'm going to do it right now. I'm going to finally say the most difficult word in this weird human vocabulary:* ***hello.***

But when her mouth opened, nothing would come out. Not a peep, not a squeak, not an anything. Sometimes she would meow, but certainly not loud enough to be heard at all.

I will try again tomorrow, Hailey confidently explained to nobody after school. *Maybe tomorrow will finally be the day.*

Tomorrow eventually came, but it took about three months and the circumstances weren't light. It started in the hallway between classes. Milkshake was curled up against a locker, sobbing a sea of tears, while a group of boys screamed and shouted slurs at them that Hailey could not believe were real.

"GET AWAY FROM THEM," Hailey screamed at the bullies, her wings fully extended across the hallway, her glistening magic wand armed and raised for battle.

The boys stopped their assault on Milkshake, but then pointed their crosshairs onto Hailey instead. Their leader lunged towards her, his hand rolling into a giant fist. His hair was about to catch on fire as sparks flew from the tips of his spikey head.

"And what are you going to do about it, FAIRY?" shouted the boy.

Hailey's face burned bright red. **FAIRY**. She hated that word. Not that there was anything wrong with being a fairy, mind you—she certainly had the wings for it. But still, a fairy was not who Hailey was. *She was a star, first and foremost, always and forever.*

Angry words bounced back and forth through Hailey's heart. *I want to teach him a lesson so he'll leave Milkshake alone*, she screamed on the inside. *Why do humans have to be so cruel to each other?*

Then it dawned on her.

Hailey lifted her magic wand upward. Magically, her feet grew ten times her size, her dress expanded, and her entire body bloomed upward, breaking through the ceiling of the school.

She looked down at the bullies. Her eyes glowed bright green.

"**EXCUSE ME**," Hailey boomed, flapping her giant wings as wooden beams from above came crashing down. "**DID YOU JUST CALL ME A FAIRY?**"

The boys screamed and scattered in every direction. Their leader peed a little in his pants, then ran away at lightspeed into a nearby hallway.

After the dust settled, Hailey shrunk down to her normal size. She climbed through the rubble and over to Milkshake. Milkshake was frozen, their face locked in a giant grin. They were still in shock at what they witnessed: ***real magic from another child just like them.***

Hailey leaned against the locker next to Milkshake, not-so-casually scooting to the floor. Neither child said a word for five whole minutes. Eventually Milkshake's face loosened and their smile faded into profound sadness.

"I hate that this happens all the time," quietly cried Milkshake. "I wish people could, or would, see the real me."

Hailey looked at Milkshake, her own eyes watering. Not being seen was something she understood intimately.

"They're just jealous," she barely squeaked, then half-smirked. "Those silly boys are itching for beautiful, minty cream hair that kinda reminds me of the most delicious sundae in the world. ***Mmmmm, chocolate mint swirl....***"

Hailey closed her eyes and started to tenderly rub her own belly. Soon after, a river of gold, sparkling slobber emerged from her lips and dripped down her chin.

Milkshake chuckled a little, then wiped some of the tears from their face.

"So, Milkshake, what's your name?" asked Hailey, still in a daze from her dessert fantasy.

"Ummm," whispered Milkshake. "Well, everybody calls me Victor, but I like to be called Violet."

"Ooooo. Is that your favorite flower? I personally love sunflowers myself," exclaimed Hailey. "But oh my gosh, violets are SO pretty. This planet is so full of such strange and wonderful things that I can barely contain myself. What about pronouns? How do you like others to think of you?"

Violet looked away from Hailey, their cheeks turning bright pink. "I like being a girl," shyly spoke the minty haired child, "and I like it when others refer to me as she."

"Well, I will call you whatever makes you feel more like you, Violet," Hailey declared, her wings fluttering in joy. "Except I might not want to call you hamburger or potato salad, or something delicious like that. But only because I would be hungry all the time and I don't really know if I want to eat you."

Violet stared blankly at Hailey. "You are weird."

"I know! Let's be friends."

After that day, Hailey and Violet became inseparable.

There were slumber parties, spy sessions, mall adventures, and freedom dances. Sometimes they even played with Hailey's magic wand, temporarily turning themselves into milkshakes, french fries, dragons, and bunny rabbits. It was the sweetest of times, for both girls. Neither child had met someone their own age who could see their hearts for what they were: *brighter and bolder than the Gaia's Sun.*

And perhaps between them, that was the strongest magical spell of all: ***love***.

But then one day, Violet disappeared. She stopped responding to Hailey's calls and texts, and seemed to have vanished from school altogether. After weeks of no contact, Hailey was devastated. *What did I do wrong?* she worried, obsessing over every little detail of the past three months. Eventually Hailey realized that this wasn't her fault at all, but her heart still hurt no less.

"I need to remember that this, too, shall pass," Hailey murmured upon the midnight sky. "I just hope that wherever Violet is, she is safe, she is protected, and she is loved."

Later that night, there was a quiet knock on the front door of her house. Hailey would have missed it entirely if it hadn't been for her magic wand amplifying the sound. She dashed downstairs to find out who could have been outside so late at night, secretly hoping her stars had been listening.

When Hailey opened the door, there was Violet. Well, it appeared to be Violet—a more boyish version of Violet, if that was even possible. She was soaking wet, drenched in the sweat of a summer storm. Her eyes were swollen red from crying and the luscious green hair that Hailey adored was gone, badly dyed, and chopped into a completely boring, double-dutch chocolate bowl cut.

"My stepmom threw out all of my clothes we bought together and told me she would never call me Violet again," sobbed the small child in the doorway. "I ran away to the only place I feel safe: *you*."

Without any hesitation, Hailey dragged Violet inside the house and into her arms. They both cried together until they couldn't. Soon after, the children raided the kitchen for a snack and retreated upstairs into more familiar territory: *Hailey's bedroom*.

"Hailey?" Violet carefully asked while digging her feet into the carpet. "Have you ever.... ummmm, have you ever felt like you were meant to be somebody, or something, different than what your parents want?"

The star princess gulped.

"Tell me more," Hailey replied, barely managing any voice at all.

"It's just...." Violet twiddled her thumbs anxiously. "For most of my life, I tried to be the perfect boy. I thought that if I could just fit in and meet everyone's expectations of who I was supposed to be, or who I thought they wanted me to be, then maybe I would change too. *Maybe I would finally be normal*."

Hailey's chin started to quiver uncontrollably. She was trying to contain how much she understood—I mean, how could she not? While she never struggled with this 'gender' thing that humans were so obsessed with, Hailey imagined it wasn't all that different from being a star in a human girl's body.

"But I didn't change," sighed Violet, her body sinking into the floor. "And everybody else, they knew it too. They continued expecting and enforcing all of these things and ideas of me that weren't me at all. Because of the way I looked. Because of my body. Because…"

"I hear you," interrupted Hailey. She gently took her best friend's hand into her own.

"I just want to be happy." Violet wiped the tears from her cheekbone. "I just want to be free to be whoever I am, however that turns out to be. It should be so simple, but it's not. Why does life have to be this way?"

"Violet." Hailey paused for a moment, barely managing the thoughts swirling over and over in her head. "Violet, what if.... what if you could be yourself all the time, everywhere, without question? Would that make your life easier?"

"Honestly? That would be like waking up from a nightmare."

With her free hand, Hailey reached out to touch Violet's face. *If I could only bring back her spark*, Hailey thought. That spark had always been so precious to her. *I wish, I want, more than anything.... for my sweet friend to be seen and loved by everyone, for everything that she is on the inside.*

"***As you wish, my love***," whispered an unexpected but familiar voice inside Hailey's heart.

In what felt like an instant, the entire room blacked out. Hailey could barely make out Violet's face, even with the moonlight still gleaming through the window. But without a moment's notice, Hailey's palm resting on Violet's cheekbone began to glow. A sparkling amber light trickled from her fingertips and danced gracefully across Violet's nose and into her big brown eyes.

Violet tried to speak, but her throat couldn't manage to squeeze a single sound. She had nothing to explain what or how she was feeling, even while watching her once beloved, shoulder length, minty hair magically grow back right in front of her eyes.

Hailey stood up and instinctively reached her hand for the ceiling. Her magic wand immediately shot upward, levitating high above her palm. Stardust emblazoned the wand's handle, and its perfectly round rose quartz core shot out a brilliant spread of rainbow magic that enveloped the girls in every direction.

"May the light of love lift the veil of her truth to everyone," confidently spoke Hailey, each word echoing across the room.

Hailey closed her eyes and listened to the deepest part of her heart, her song, soaring through the air. Her entire body glistened brighter than ever before.

Suddenly, a bright beam of light burst through the wand and poured itself into Violet's chest. Her skin and hair began glowing brighter and more colorful than Hailey herself, and her body skyrocketed up through the ceiling and into another dimension. A lavender and bright blue nebula swirled around Violet until her whole being was cocooned in what could best be described as pure love.

Stars exploded in every direction. Light poured from the tips of Violet's fingers, toes, and head. She screamed not in fear, but with hope. Her wardrobe, her skin, her everything—all that she felt trapped in—melted away and uncovered something new, something real. Finally and forever, Violet was unlocked. *She was free.*

The lights turned back on. Hailey's bedroom quickly returned to normal, as if nothing magical happened at all. But something did happened, something that surprised them both.

As Violet glanced into the mirror, her now magically charged, hazel-blue eyes widened brightly. There was a twinkle now, a softness that she had never seen before.

"I'm... I'm... I'm beautiful," gasped Violet. "You've made me.... beautiful."

Hailey gently took her best friend's hand and squeezed it softly.

"No, my sweet Violet, you made yourself beautiful. You were always beautiful. *We just made it a little easier for the rest of the world to see what we knew all along."*

Both girls lept into each other's arms. It was a collision of love, kinda like a supernova of two hearts blazing across the midnight sky. They stood there, hand in hand, for what felt like hours and probably until the end of time.

From that night onward, Violet was forever changed. Nobody questioned her name or gender again, even after she decided to not have a gender at all.

As for Hailey and Violet, they remained the best of friends. Wherever they went and whomever they met, both shined their love and beamed with pride, "**Hello world! We are Hailey and Violet, starhearts of the light,** ***the Sisters from the Stars.***"

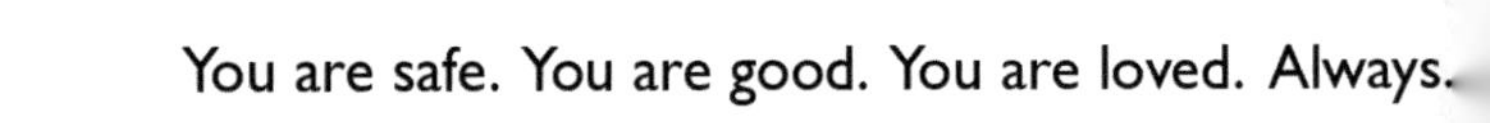
You are safe. You are good. You are loved. Always.

About the Author:
Amy Eleanor Heart

my Heart is a queer storyteller nd social justice advocate. She is ctively fighting for the rights of ransgender girls and non-binary ids everywhere.

rom 2002 to 2013, Amy worked xclusively in non-profit community elevision as both educator and rganizer. Since then, she has ocused her energy on 'unlearning' hite supremacy, studying disability stice, and building stronger elationships with other trans omen. Amy has a Bachelor's of Fine rts in Film Studies from University f California, Santa Barbara.

Vhen Amy isn't organizing, she is robably looking after a number of eloved children in her life. Amy urrently lives in Olympia, WA.

CPSIA information can be obtained
at www.ICGtesting.com
Printed in the USA
LVHW07n2319130718
583688LV00002B/3/P